MOON
TIGER

MOON TIGER

TIGER

By Phyllis Root
Art by Ed Young

Holt, Rinehart and Winston · New York

Mom is mad at me again, and it's all Michael's fault. Just because I wouldn't read him a story, he went crying to Mom. I tried to tell her I was busy building a house for my tiger, but she wouldn't listen.

"Jessica Ellen," she said in that voice she uses when I lose my mittens or don't want to take a bath, "if you can't help me by reading to your little brother, you can go straight to bed."

So here it is, Michael's bedtime, and I have to go to bed too, even though I'm seven and he's only four. It's all his fault.

Maybe a tiger will come through the window, first one paw on the sill, then the other, and then his head with its furry ears. A huge tiger—a moon tiger with black stripes and big, yellow eyes.

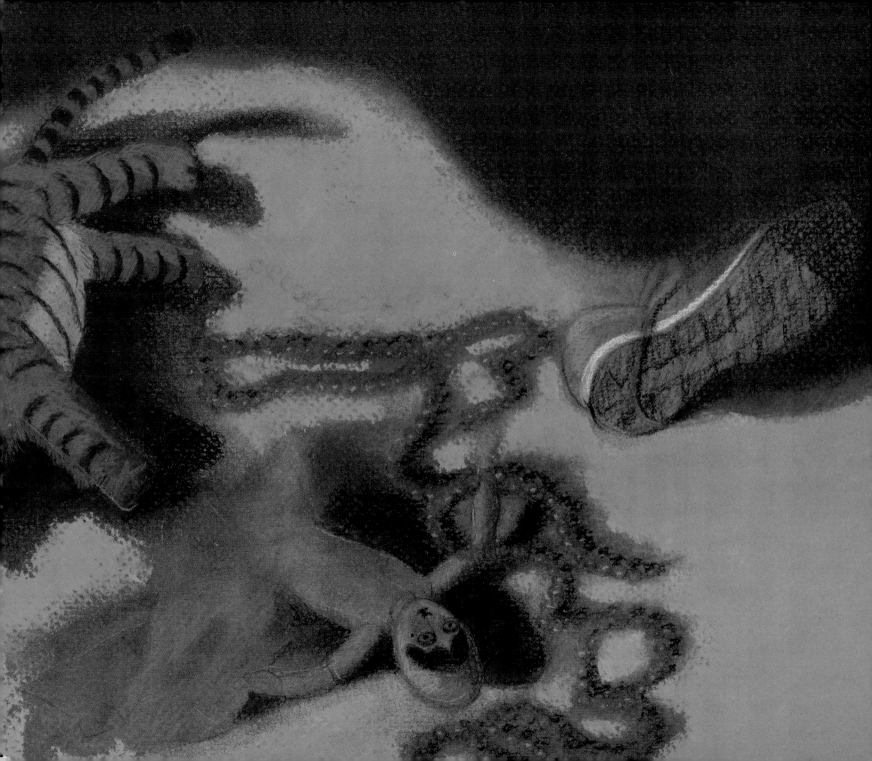

He'll look all around the room, and then he'll leap across the moonbeams and over to my bed. He'll hardly make a sound, but I'll hear him.

Michael will be asleep. If he saw the moon tiger, he'd probably cry. But not me—I'll be brave. Tigers don't scare me.

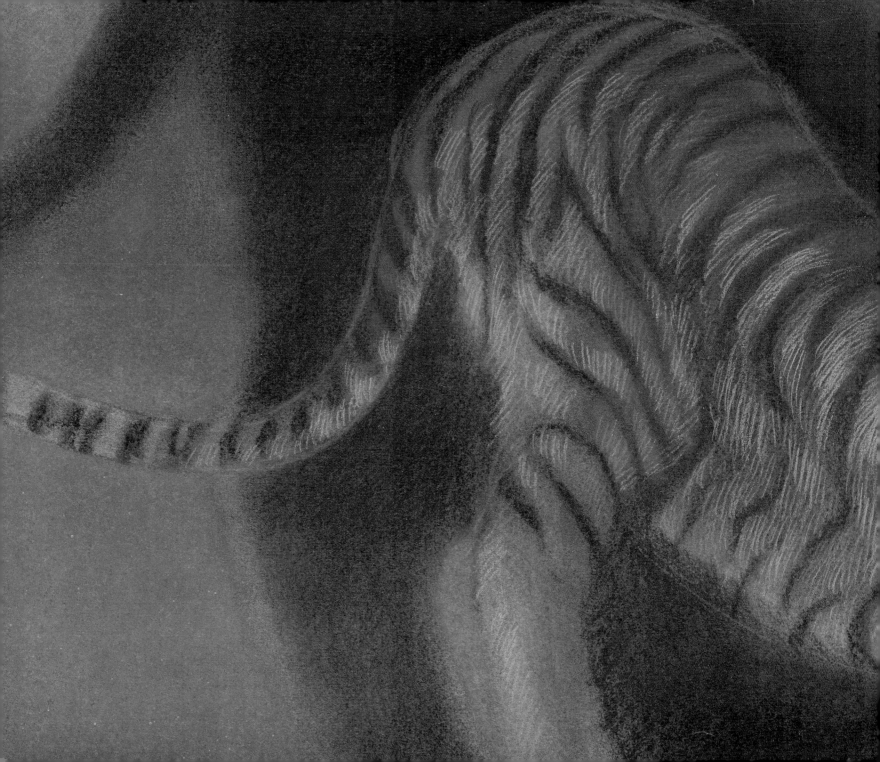

"Hello, moon tiger," I'll say, and I'll scratch his enormous ears and stroke his long, striped back. He'll purr deep in his chest and rub his head against my knees. Then, with his front paws out and his tail behind, he'll stretch and stretch and *stretch* until he almost fills up the whole room.

I'll jump on his back, and we'll fly into the night with tremendous leaps.

First, we'll search for polar bears at the north pole. It will be cold — so cold my breath would freeze into snowflakes if I weren't nestled deep in the tiger's fur.

Next, we'll bound over forests and mountains and oceans on our way to the wilds of Africa. We'll follow gorilla tracks deep into the center of the jungle, and maybe I'll even see a real hippopotamus along the way.

Then maybe, if I get sleepy, I'll tell the moon tiger to take me home. Michael will still be asleep.

"That's my little brother," I'll say, sliding off the tiger's back. "He's such a baby. He cries all the time and gets me in trouble."

The moon tiger will sniff him with his cold, black nose.

"Do you want me to eat him?" he'll ask.

I'll think about it for a while. If Michael were gone, I wouldn't be in trouble all the time. I wouldn't have to read to him or share my toys or take him fishing with me. But Mom and Dad might miss him. And sometimes it's fun to tell him stories I've made up or to show him what I learned in school.

"I guess not," I'll say. "After all, he's just a little kid. He doesn't know any better about crying. Maybe I can teach him."

"Maybe you can," the moon tiger will say.

"Tomorrow when he wakes up, I'll tell him all about you, moon tiger. And maybe next time, if he's brave like me and doesn't cry, he can come too."

"Maybe he can," the moon tiger will answer.

Then, after licking my face with his long, scratchy tongue, he'll turn and spring to the window.

"Good-bye, moon tiger," I'll call, snuggling deep under the covers. "Come back soon."

"Maybe I will," the moon tiger will say, disappearing over the windowsill with a flick of his tail. And as I fall asleep his words will float back through the window, big and round and yellow, "sometime soon."

Phyllis Root was born in Fort Wayne, Indiana. A graduate of Valparaiso University in Valparaiso, Indiana, she is now a free-lance writer, and author of several children's books, including *Soup for Supper,* published by Harper and Row. Phyllis Root lives in Minneapolis, Minnesota, with her husband, Jim, and her daughters, Amelia and Ellen.

Ed Young was born in China and spent his childhood in Shanghai. After coming to the United States, he studied at the University of Illinois and at the Art Center in Los Angeles. The illustrator of many children's books, he has received many awards for his work, including a Caldecott Honor. His book *Up a Tree* was selected by *The New York Times* as one of the ten best illustrated books for 1983. Ed Young now lives in Hastings-on-Hudson, New York.

For Jim
and for Amelia
—P.R.

For Filomena Tuosto
—E.Y.

Text copyright © 1985 by Phyllis Root
Illustrations copyright © 1985 by Ed Young
All rights reserved, including the right to reproduce this
book or portions thereof in any form.
Published by Holt, Rinehart and Winston,
383 Madison Avenue, New York, New York 10017.
Published simultaneously in Canada by Holt, Rinehart and
Winston of Canada, Limited.
Library of Congress Cataloging in Publication Data
Root, Phyllis.
Moon tiger.
Summary: After getting in trouble because of her
little brother Michael, Jessica Ellen imagines a visit
from a wonderful giant tiger who can take her flying
through the night or eat Michael.
1. Children's stories, American.   [1. Tigers—Fiction.
2. Imagination—Fiction.   3. Brothers and sisters—Fiction]
I. Young, Ed, ill.   II. Title.
PZ7.R6784Mo 1985   [E]   85-7572
ISBN: 0-03-000042-4

First Edition

Designed by Amy Hill
Printed in Japan
10 9 8 7 6 5 4 3 2 1

ISBN 0-03-000042-4